The Seven Stones of Sligo

An Irish Legend

The Seven Stones of Sligo

An Irish Legend

Retold by Helen Boswell-Smith

Illustrated by Margaret Power

Rigby PM Collection and PM Plus
Ruby Level 27

U.S. Edition © 2006 Harcourt Achieve Inc.
10801 N. MoPac Expressway
Building #3
Austin, TX 78759
www.harcourtachieve.com

Text © 2001 Cengage Learning Australia Pty Limited
Illustrations © 2001 Cengage Learning Australia Pty Limited
Originally published in Australia by Cengage Learning Australia

9 10 11 12 13 14 15   1957   14 13 12 11 10
4500219090

Text: Helen Boswell-Smith
Illustrations: Margaret Power
Printed in China by 1010 Printing International Ltd

The Seven Stones of Sligo
ISBN 978 0 76 357786 5

Contents

Chapter 1

The Beginning

Imagine a patchwork land of the greenest rolling fields you will ever see, stitched together by low stone walls. A land of ancient hills clouded in misty rain, where the waves have crashed and swirled against the rocks of rugged shores for centuries, and woodlands are filled with bluebells and primroses that bloom in the spring. Such a land is Ireland.

Ireland is a land of magic. It has myths and legends and stories of little people, like fairies and leprechauns, as well as great monsters and serpents. Irish people are so gifted at telling their stories that sometimes it is hard to believe they are not true. Take the story of the seven stones of Sligo, for example.

Sligo is the main town in County Sligo, in the western part of Ireland. Just outside the town of Sligo, on a hill overlooking the town, are the ruins of an ancient castle. When you look at that castle, it's hard to believe that a mermaid once lived there a long, long time ago.

Chapter 2

Once Upon a Time

The story begins with a young prince growing up in that castle. His father was the chieftain—and very powerful he was, too. His chiefdom stretched across all of Connaught, which was a very large part of Ireland. The young prince was extremely handsome. He was tall and strong and had a fine head of fiery red hair.

Many other chieftains had suggested that the prince marry their daughters, but the old chieftain could not bear the thought of losing his son's companionship. You see, the prince's mother had died when he was born and the prince and his father were very close.

Throughout his childhood and youth, the prince had been at his father's side, learning how to be the next chieftain of all Connaught.

Sadly, the old chieftain became ill and died, leaving the prince to grieve for his father, who was also his closest friend. The prince became the great chieftain. But he was alone with all his wealth and his servants and his power, and he would gladly have given half of all this away for a loving companion.

Other chieftains offered their daughters in marriage, but in spite of his loneliness, the young chieftain could not bring himself to marry someone he did not love.

Chapter 3

The Lonely Chieftain

The prince began to take long walks over the hills and the valleys of County Sligo searching for what, he did not know. He loved the sound of the waves crashing onto the rocky shores of Sligo Bay, and would sit for hour after hour on the clifftop watching the ocean and listening to the sound of the ocean's roar as it smashed against the rocks.

On one such day, one beautiful golden day, he sat watching the sea, which sparkled as if a sackful of diamonds had been tossed onto the water. While watching the waves, the young chieftain noticed a movement on one of the rocks below.

At first he thought it was a trick of his imagination, but then he saw it again. Something was moving on the rock. Was it a seal basking in the sunshine? Was it a dolphin cast up on the rocks? He moved closer to gain a better look, being careful to keep himself hidden so as not to scare the creature.

To his amazement, when he came close, he could see it was a young woman, sitting on the rock, combing her hair. She was the most beautiful creature the young chieftain had ever seen. Her long golden hair fell below her waist, where she was wearing a slim-fitting skirt.

The young chieftain looked again and realized that it was not a skirt at all, but the tail of a fish. The beautiful young woman was a mermaid!

The young man remained hidden, for he did not want to frighten the mermaid, and eventually she slipped from the rock and swam away.

Chapter 4

Falling in Love

The next day the young chieftain went again to the same spot on the clifftop in the hope of seeing the mermaid. Sure enough, there she was, but this time as she combed her hair, she sang a soft tune, the sweetest he had ever heard.

The young man was enraptured and instantly fell in love with the mermaid. But he dared not reveal himself to her in case she swam away and never came back.

So, each day he returned to the clifftop above Sligo Bay to watch the beautiful mermaid comb her hair and sing songs in the purest of voices.

One day, when he arrived at the clifftop, he was surprised to see the mermaid lying sound asleep. Over her lay a shawl spun from all the colors of the sea. Now, the young chieftain knew enough about mermaids to know that if he could take the shawl from the mermaid and put it where she could not see it, she would lose her fish tail and become a woman.

He crept closer and closer to his beloved while she slept, and at last he was near enough to gently lift the shawl off her sleeping body. He quickly folded the shawl and hid it inside his own tunic. Then he sat quietly and waited for the mermaid to wake.

Chapter 5

The Happy Family

Eventually, the mermaid stirred and opened her eyes. At first she was startled to see the young chieftain, but he held out his hand to her and spoke in gentle tones, and she knew that she had no need to be afraid.

When she looked down to where her fish tail should have been, she saw that she had legs and feet instead. The chieftain begged her to go back with him to his castle. He asked her to become his wife and help him to rule over all of Connaught.

The mermaid could see what a good and kind man the young chieftain was and agreed to marry him. She went back to the castle with him and they were married with great rejoicing and much dancing.

But the young chieftain knew the power of the shawl and the sea. He knew if his wife ever saw her shawl again, she would turn back into a mermaid and all would be lost. So he kept the shawl hidden in a hollow tree, a long way from the castle.

As time passed, the couple was blessed with a child—a beautiful daughter just like her mother. Then a son was born with the same fine red hair as his father. Before long, there were seven children running and laughing in the castle, their playful shouts filling the air with joyfulness.

The chieftain and his wife could not have been happier.

Chapter 6

The Secret Spot

One day, when their youngest child was four years old, the chieftain took him to visit another prince who lived a long way from the castle. On the way, they passed the tree where the shawl was hidden, and the chieftain was shocked to see that the tree had been struck by lightning and was lying in the field.

Worried that the shawl might be discovered, the chieftain took it and buried it nearby. Then he rolled a stone over the top to mark the spot.

The child watched in silence. He saw the shawl his father buried and could not forget its beautiful colors.

That night, when his mother came to kiss him goodnight and sing him a lullaby, he told her what he had seen.

The chieftain's wife became very sad. Huge tears rolled down her cheeks, for now that the shawl's hiding place had been revealed to her, she knew she must find it and return to the sea. For once the shawl was unearthed she would most certainly turn back into a mermaid, and the sea would take back all she'd had on land.

The saddened woman spent the whole of that night crying, for she loved her husband and children and could not bear the thought of what was about to happen.

Chapter 7

Saying Good-bye

Early the next morning, the wife took the seven children and walked with them to where the shawl lay buried under the stone. The youngest child, not realizing the consequences of his actions, showed his mother where the shawl was buried.

With a heavy heart, the children's mother asked them to help her push aside the stone and there, beneath a covering of earth, she found her shawl.

The chieftain's wife picked up the shawl and walked with her children to the seashore, where she bade them all to stand in the shallows of the bay.

She put the shawl around her shoulders and began to sing a song of heartbreaking sadness. As she did so, she embraced each of her children. And at the touch of the shawl, each child turned into stone.

Finally, the chieftain's wife wrapped the shawl around her own hips and immediately her legs disappeared. In their place was her fish tail.

With one last sob, she slid into the ocean and swam away, never to be seen again.

Chapter 8

Alone Again

The chieftain was distraught at the loss of his wife and children. For a long time, he had no idea where they had gone. In his grief, he took to wandering the hills and valleys again. It was on one of those walks that he came across the fallen tree and the nearby stone.

When he dug into the earth and found nothing, he knew what must have happened to his wife.

He ran to the clifftop, and on seeing the seven new stones in Sligo Bay, he realized that his children were also lost to him forever.

The chieftain abandoned the castle where he and his family had been so happy. He could no longer bear to live there.

He gave up his powerful position as chieftain and went to live in a little stone cottage near the clifftop, so he could be near his wife and children, should they ever return to him.

But they never did.